한 줄의 시 심다

한 줄의 시

삶

유 창 근 시집

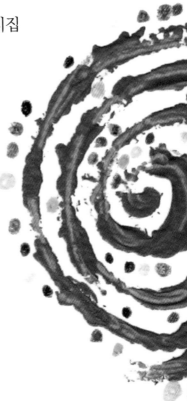

도서
출판 문현

요즘 관심을 모으고 있는
미니픽션 Minifiction의 길이가
엽서 한 장을 넘지 않는다.
그렇다면 詩를 굳이
길게 써야 할 이유가 있을까?

참으로 오랜시간 고민을 하다가
몇년 전 부터 한 행짜리 詩를 써왔다.

人生이란 어차피
하나의 부호에 지나지 않을 뿐인데
말 많은 것도 죄라는 생각이다.

예쁜에셀의 하나님께 감사드린다.

이천 십년 새 아침에

가을의 미토스 Autumn's mythos

가을 Autumn   12

낙엽 Fallen leaves   14

인생 Life   16

십자가 A cross   18

자화상 A self-portrait   20

절망 Despair   22

입소문 Word of mouth   24

석양 Sunset   26

난풍 Fall foliage   28

권력에게 To Power   30

욕망 A desire   32

종점에서 In a terminal   34

트라 우마 Trauma   36

유서 A will   38

허상 虛像 A virtual image   40

한계 限界 A limit   42

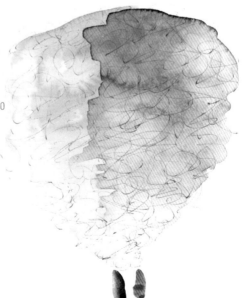

겨울의 미토스 Winter's Mythos

일탈 逸脫 A deviation　46

아웃사이더 An outsider　48

설산 雪山 A snow mountain　50

그믐달 The old moon　52

쓰레기통 A trash can　54

구토 Vomiting　56

가시밭길 A thorny path　58

침묵 Silence　60

지하철 A subway　62

성격 차이 A personality clash　64

정체 停滯 Congestion　66

동굴 A cave　68

잔머리 Petty tricks　70

유전무죄 有錢無罪 Money talks　72

마지막 기도 The last pray　74

궤변 詭辯 Sphistries　76

터널 A tunnel　78

걸림돌 An obstacle　80

죽음 Death　82

봄의 미토스 Spring' s mythos

사랑 Love   86

카타르시스 Catharsis   88

꽃샘추위 The last cold snap   90

옹달샘 A small spring   92

개화기 開花期 Flowering season   94

분기점 A turning point   96

금잔디 Golden turf   98

보고 싶다 Want to see   100

추억 Memories   102

곱슬머리 Curly hair   104

여유 Relaxation   106

낯선 방 An unfamiliar room   108

비 맞은 새 A soaked bird   110

하늘 문 Heaven's door   112

아버지 Father   114

오페라하우스 An Opera House   116

오해 A misunderstanding   118

회개 Repentance   120

여름의 미토스 Summer's mythos

배꼽티 A bare midriff 124

보름달 A full moon 126

구름 Cloud 128

무지개 Rainbow 130

금강 Geum river 132

욕심 Greed 134

위선 僞善 Hypocrisy 136

역류 Detention 138

이드 Id 140

사막에서 In a desert 142

성숙 Growing 144

폭포 A waterfall 146

미니스커트 A miniskirt 148

비 오는 날 A raining day 150

잡초 Weed 152

테헤란로 Teheran road 154

포클레인 An excavator 156

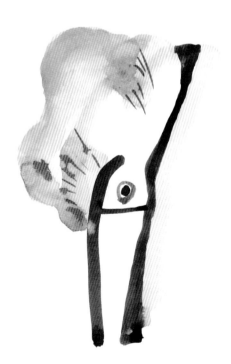

가을의 미토스 Autumn's mythos

가을 Autumn 12

낙엽 Fallen leaves 14

인생 Life 16

십자가 A cross 18

자화상 A self-portrait 20

절망 Despair 22

입소문 Word of mouth 24

석양 Sunset 26

단풍 Fall foliage 28

권력에게 To Power 30

욕망 A desire 32

종점에서 In a terminal 34

트라 우마 Trauma 36

유서 A will 38

허상 虛像 A virtual image 40

한계 限界 A limit 42

가을 Autumn

늙은 女流詩人의 손에 잡힌 구름 한 점

A piece of cloud on hands of an old lady poet

낙엽 Fallen leaves

청소부의 빗자루에 매달려 몸부림치는 更年期

Struggling menopause hanging on the sweeper's broom

인생 Life

끊임없는 가지치기
Endless pruning

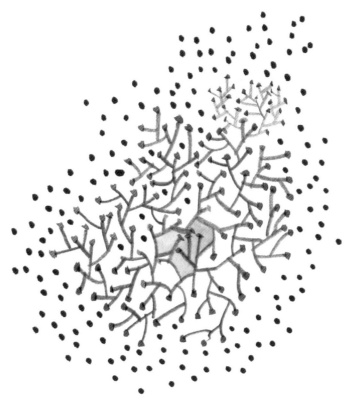

십자가

A cross

구
겨
진

심장이

첨탑위에서

바람개비처럼 돌고 있다.

A crumpled heart is spinning on the steeple like a windmill.

자화상

A self-portrait

거울 한구석에 구부정히 서 있는 소나무

A pine tree standing crooked on the corner of a mirror

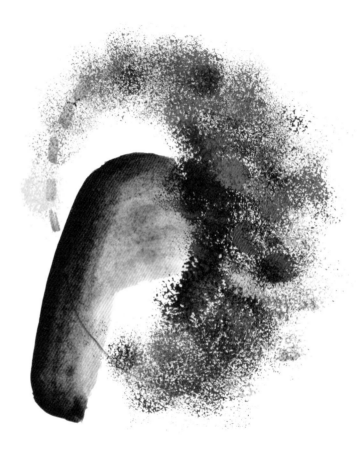

절망 Despair

쉼표들의 마지막 숨쉬기

The last breathing of the rests

입소문 Word of mouth

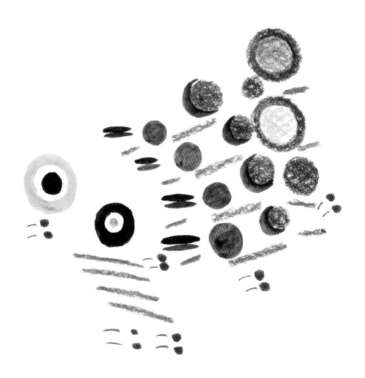

말 말 말 말 … 그놈의 주둥아리

Talk, talk, talk … What a hole!

석양 Sunset

산마루 나뭇가지에 수줍게 매달린 홍시

A bashful soft persimmon hanging under the branch over the
mountain ridge

단풍 Fall foliage

농익은 가을이 용광로에서 끓고 있다

Overripe autumn is boiling in a blast furnace.

권력에게 To Power

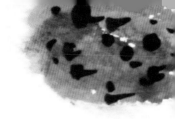

뜰때 날아라

Fly when popular.

욕망 A desire

슨식간에 시들어 버리는 안개꽃

Babies' breath withering in a flash

종점에서 In a terminal

이제 모두 떠났구나

Everything departs away now!

트라우마 Trauma

초침 끝에이 깊이 패는 생채기

A scratch deeply caved in at the end of the second hand

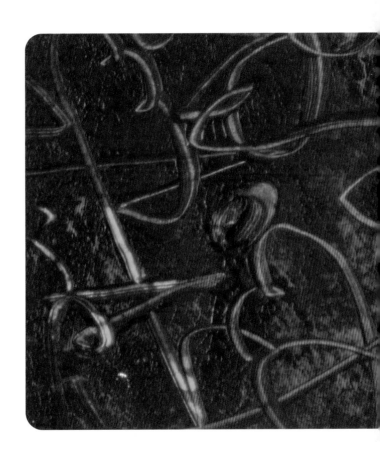

미안해, 미안해…

I'm so so so sorry.

유서 A will

허상 虛像 A virtual image

쇼 윈도 안에서 의연히 팔짱끼고 서 있는 마네킹 부부

A mannequin couple standing arm-in-arm with dignity in a show window

한계 限界 A limit

에라, 모르겠다 Oh my, Que Sera Sera.

겨울의 미토스 Winter`s Mythos

일탈 逸脫 A deviation   46

아웃사이더 An outsider   48

설산 雪山 A snow mountain   50

그믐달 The old moon   52

쓰레기통 A trash can   54

구토 Vomiting   56

가시밭길 A thorny path   58

침묵 Silence   60

지하철 A subway   62

성격 차이 A personality clash   64

정체 停滯 Congestion   66

동굴 A cave   68

잔머리 Petty tricks   70

유전무죄 有錢無罪 Money talks   72

마지막 기도 The last pray   74

궤변 詭辯 Sphistries   76

터널 A tunnel   78

걸림돌 An obstacle   80

죽음 Death   82

일탈 逸脫 A deviation

청바지 입고 산책나온 겨울 허수아비

A walking winterly puppet in blue jeans

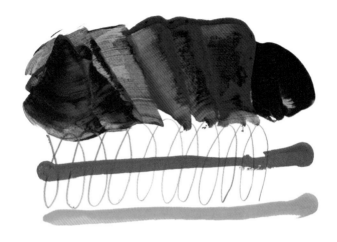

상처난 자존심이 정신병원 앞에서 다리를 절고 있다

Wounded pride hobbles in front of a mental hospital.

아웃사이더
An outsider

설산 雪山 A snow mountain

햇솜을 덮고 누운 알래스카 백곰

An Alaskan polar bear lying down under clean cotton

그믐달 The old moon

빈민촌 낡은 지붕 위에 비스듬히 누워 있는 우수 憂愁

Melancholy lying askew on the old roof in slurbs

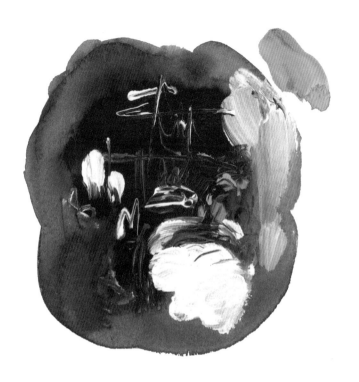

쓰레기통 A trash can

더불어 오염될까봐 비껴간다

Steer past for fear of being polluted together

 구토 Vomiting

박쥐의 불비물에 절여진 비곗덩어리들

Fat lumps preserved in excrement of bats

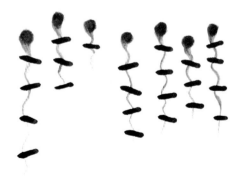

가시밭길

A thorny path

서로의 조용한 절규가 있다

絶叫

There is mutual silent exclamation.

침묵 Silence

되돌릴 수 없는 마지막 폐쇄 회로

A last closed circuit that cannot be restored

지하철 A subway

무울한 날이면 전설처럼 동굴 속으로 역주행한다

On a gloomy day, drive the wrong way into a cave like legend.

성격 차이 A personality clash

영원히 合流할 수 없는 평행선 [拮]

Parallel lines that cannot meet forever

정체 停滯 Congestion

고속도로가 온종일 동맥경화증으로 신음한다

A Superhighway groans with arteriosclerosis all day.

동굴 A cave

산허리에 숨어있는 갈색 호기심

Brown curiosity lurking in a mountainside

A mosaic of the meanest words

가장 비열한 言語들의 모자이크

잔머리 Petty tricks

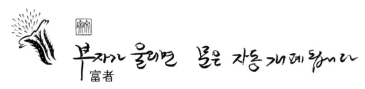

富者

If rich person rings, the door opens and shuts automatically.

유전무죄

有錢無罪　Money talks

마지막 기도 The last pray

베풀며 살다가 잠자듯 떠나게 하소서

O Lord, let me live merciful life and leave this world as sleep.

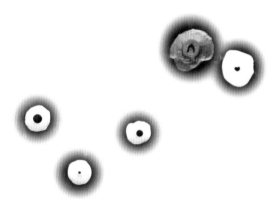

二重人格者들이 내놓은 상습적 옐로카드

Conformed yellow card that two-faced persons pull out

궤변 詭辯 Sophistries

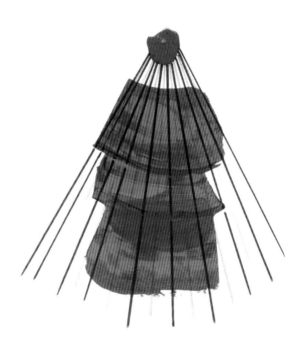

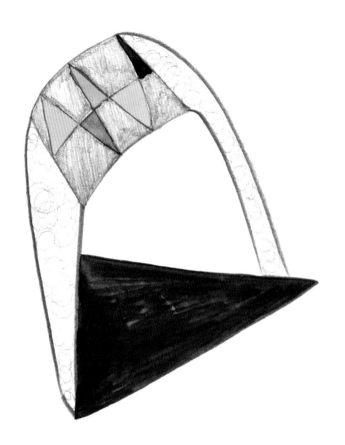

터널 A tunnel

금방 터질것 같다 [印]

Seems like to burst right away

설 자리도 모르는 늗치 덩어리

All slow-witted lump who doesn't know where to keep his footing

걸림돌
An obstacle

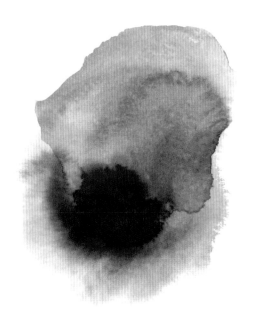

죽음 Death

Period

봄의 미토스 Spring's mythos

사랑 Love   86

카타르시스 Catharsis   88

꽃샘추위 The last cold snap   90

옹달샘 A small spring   92

개화기 開花期 Flowering season   94

분기점 A turning point   96

금잔디 Golden turf   98

보고 싶다 Want to see   100

추억 Memories   102

곱슬머리 Curly hair   104

여유 Relaxation   106

낯선 방 An unfamiliar room   108

비 맞은 새 A soaked bird   110

하늘 문 Heaven's door   112

아버지 Father   114

오페라하우스 An Opera House   116

오해 A misunderstanding   118

회개 Repentance   120

사랑 Love

서로 눈물 닦아주기 To wipe each other's tears

카타르시스 Catharsis

南江 대 숲에 안개비로 내리던 봄의 미토스

Spring's mythos that drop by mist in the Namgang bamboo grove

꽃샘추위 The last cold snap

어린 봄이 꽃잎 위에서 떨고 있다

The young spring is trembling on a petal.

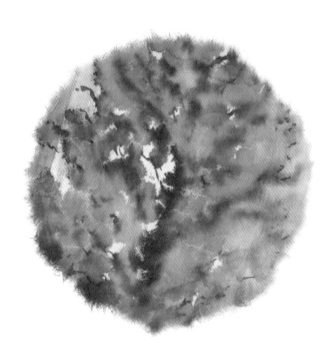

옹달샘 A small spring

Silence that shrinks from the light touching of breath

개화기

開花期　Flowering season

우리 보다 더 요란하게 터지는 꽃망울 소리

Sounds of the flower buds that burst more noisily than thunder

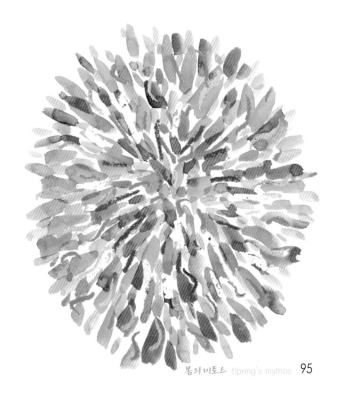

분기점 A turning point

方向이 다를때 군말없이 갈라서는 길이 참 멋지다

When direction is different, the way that separate without
unnecessary remark is really nice.

금잔디

Golden turf

숲바닥 하나로도 가려지는 외인출입 금지구역

Foreigners keep-out area covered with just one palm

보고 싶다

Want to see

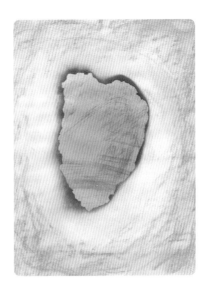

유년의 강가에 새겨놓은 모래 발자국

Footprint craving on riverside sands in one's childhood

추억 Memories

그 때가 참 좋았어 Those days were really good.

곱슬머리
Curly hair

最初의 지연산 民主主義

First natural democracy

여유 Relaxation

연둣빛 이파리 사이로 고개 내민 보드라운 햇살

Soft sunbeam that stick out head through yellowish green leaves

낯선 방 An unfamiliar room

들어오세요, 천천히 !!

Enter, slowly.

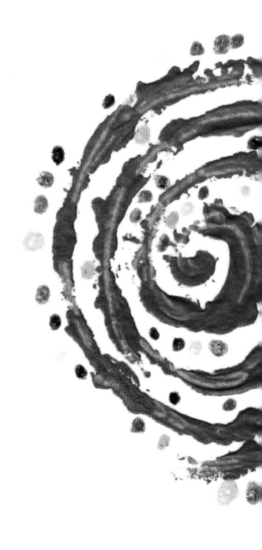

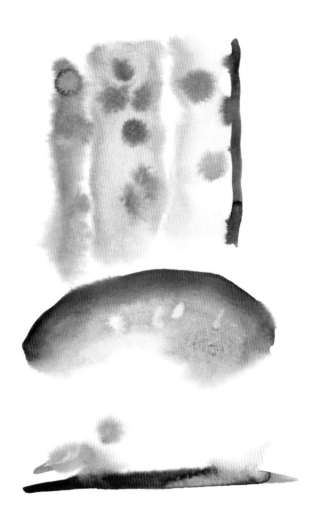

비 맞은 새 A soaked bird

훨훨 날고 싶다

Want to fly freely

하늘 문 Heaven's door

성숙한 빛들이 현란하게 질주하는 통로

A passageway where matured lights speed

아버지 Father

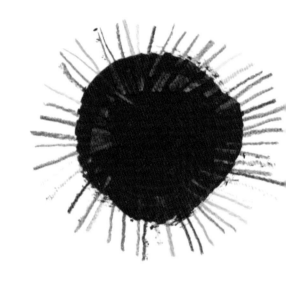

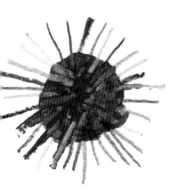

기대고 싶다 Want to lean on

오페라하우스

An Opera House

지진도 멈추게 한 그 목소리 🔴

The voice that stops even the earthquakes

때가 되면 말겠지 [印]

In due time, it will tell its own tale.

오해 A misunderstanding

정말 죄송해요

I am really sorry.

회개 Repentance

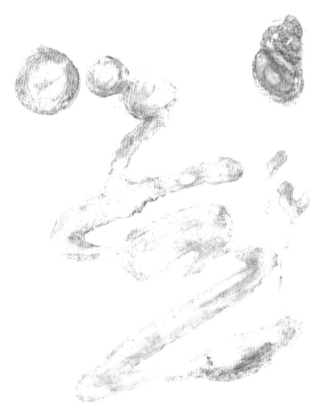

여름의 미토스 Summer's mythos

배꼽티 A bare midriff 124

보름달 A full moon 126

구름 Cloud 128

무지개 Rainbow 130

금강 Geum river 132

욕심 Greed 134

위선 僞善 Hypocrisy 136

역류 Detention 138

이드 Id 140

사막에서 In a desert 142

성숙 Growing 144

폭포 A waterfall 146

미니스커트 A miniskirt 148

비 오는 날 A raining day 150

잡초 Weed 152

테헤란로 Teheran road 154

포클레인 An excavator 156

배꼽티 A bare midriff

참외 밭에서 갓 올라온 성성한 나르시시즘

Live narcissism which freshly rise in a melon field

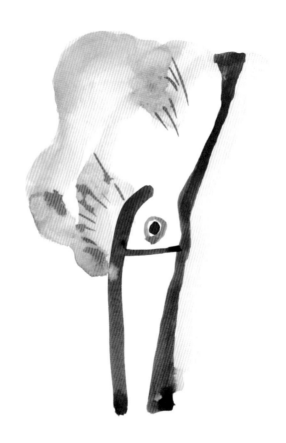

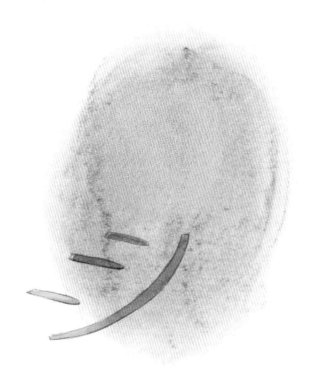

보름달 A full moon

恋人들이 쏘아올린 금빛 애드벌룬

A golden color advertising balloon which lovers shoot up

구름 Cloud

냇물 속으로 헬리콥터가 천천히 헤엄쳐 간다

A helicopter slowly swims deep into a stream.

무지개 Rainbow

열아홉살 풋내 나는 색동저고리

A girl's jacket with sleeves of multicolored stripes and
a smell of fresh nineteen-year-old greens

금강 Geum River

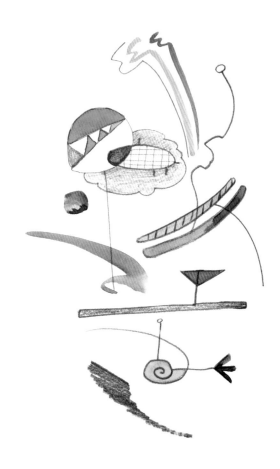

밤꽃 香氣에 취한 六月이 구름으로 떠간다

June that get drunken with the odor of chestnut blossoms floats away as a cloud.

욕심  Greed

 더, 더, 더, 더⋯

More and more and more ⋯

위선
偽善 Hypocrisy

샤넬 香水로 둥장한 마대걸레

A mop disguised with Chanel

역류 Detention

늙은 수직선이 말없이 위험수위를 내려다보고 있다

Old perpendicular line is looking down the dangerous
water level silently.

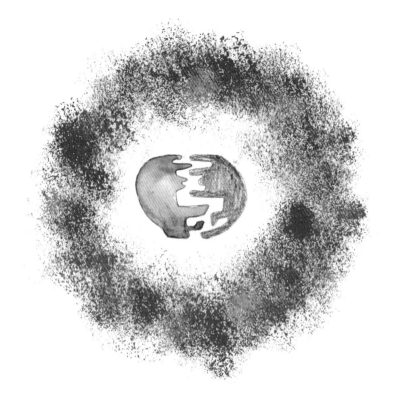

이 드 Id

예측불허의 오만덩어리

A clod of unpredictable snobbish

사막에서 In a desert

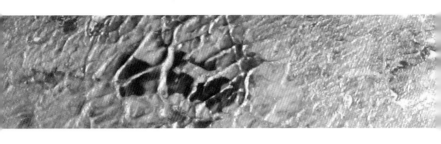

실핏줄까지 멈출것 같다

Even the thread veins is likely to be blocked.

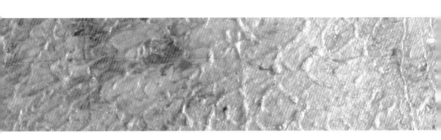

성숙 Growing

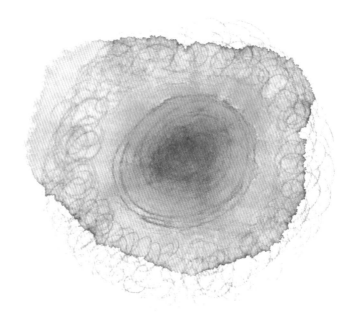

나이 만큼 빈 자리 만들어 가기

Making empty room as many as one's ages

폭포 A waterfall

긴 혓바닥을 내밀어 온갖 소리를 핥고 있다

Sucking up every sound with its long tongue lolling out

열 받으면 올라가는 아슬아슬한 수은주

A mercury rising breathtakingly when heated

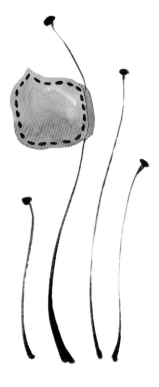

미니스커트 A miniskirt

비 오는 날 A raining day

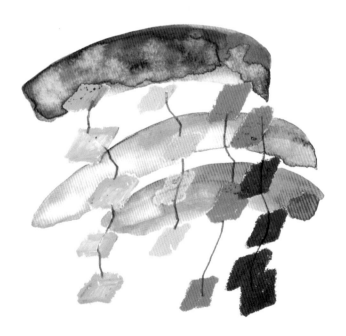

한 줄의 詩, 심다

우산 좀 씌워주세요

Share your umbrella, please.

잠초  Weed

욕심만 먹고사는 동물성 에고이스트

Animal egoist devouring only greed

테헤란로 Teheran road

구멍난 위조지폐들이 네온사인에 잡혀 파닥거린다

Fake notes with holes caught by neon sign are flopping.

포클레인 An excavator

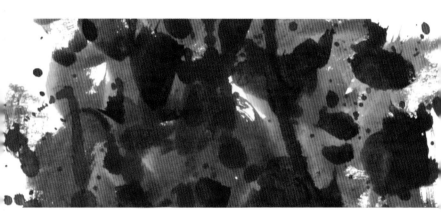

가진 것 없이 힘만 센 돌대가리

An idiot with nothing but strength

유 창 근 兪昌根

충남 부여에서 태어나 시인, 문학평론가로 등단하였다.
현재 문학박사이며 문예창작학과 교수로 재직 중이다.
시집『둘이서』, 평론집『문학과 인생』,『문학의 흐름』,『한국 현대시의 위상』,
이론서『문학을 보는 눈』,『문학비평연구』 등 40여권의 저서가 있다.
제1회 조국문학상(평론 부문)을 비롯하여 여러 차례 문학상을 받았다.

E-mail rootpia24@hanmail.net
Mobile 010-3360-7585   연구실 02-300-1222

한 줄의 시

俞 昌 根 詩集, 싶다

인 쇄	2010년 1월 2일
발 행	2010년 1월 5일
지은이	유 창 근
펴낸이	한 신 규
펴낸곳	도서출판 문헌
	서울특별시 송파구 문정동 99-10 장지빌딩 303호
	T.02.443.0211 F.02.443.0212 E-mail.mun2009@naver.com
등 록	2009년 2월 24일(제2009-14호)

ISBN   978-89-94131-04-7   03810
정 가   11,000원